RICHARD PLATT is a renowned non-fiction writer whose previous titles include *Pirate Diary* (Walker) illustrated by Chris Riddell, which won the 2002 Kate Greenaway Medal. Its predecessor, *Castle Diary,* was shortlisted for the same prize as well as for the Kurt Maschler Award and the *History Today* prize. His collaboration with Stephen Biesty led to half a dozen books in the Cross-Sections series for Dorling Kindersley: the first, *Incredible Cross Sections*, was shortlisted for the Smarties Prize, and the last, *Incredible Body*, for the Rhône Poulenc Prize. He has written twenty other other titles for DK including *Cinema, Pirate* and *Spy* in the Eyewitness Guides series, and *Everest* and *Aztec* in the Eyewitness Discovery series.

RUPERT VAN WYK is a widely-travelled illustrator whose books include *A Song for Planet Earth*, written by Meredith Hooper (OUP, 1999), *Sharks* (OUP, 2000) and *The Kickstart Students' Book* (OUP, 2001). Working on *The Vanishing Rainforest* has inspired him to visit South America and see the rainforest for himself.

For Hamish, Freya and Elissa – R.P.

First published in Great Britain in 2003 by
Frances Lincoln Limited, 4 Torriano Mews
Torriano Avenue, London NW5 2RZ
www.franceslincoln.com

First paperback edition 2004

British Library Cataloguing in Publication Data
available on request

ISBN 0-7112-1960-5 hardback
ISBN 0-7112-2170-7 paperback

Set in Stone Sans Semibold
Printed in Singapore

1 3 5 7 9 8 6 4 2

Find out how you can help to save the planet
by visiting www.wildlifebiz.org/bellamy_good_news/

The Vanishing Rainforest

RICHARD PLATT

Illustrated by RUPERT VAN WYK

FRANCES LINCOLN

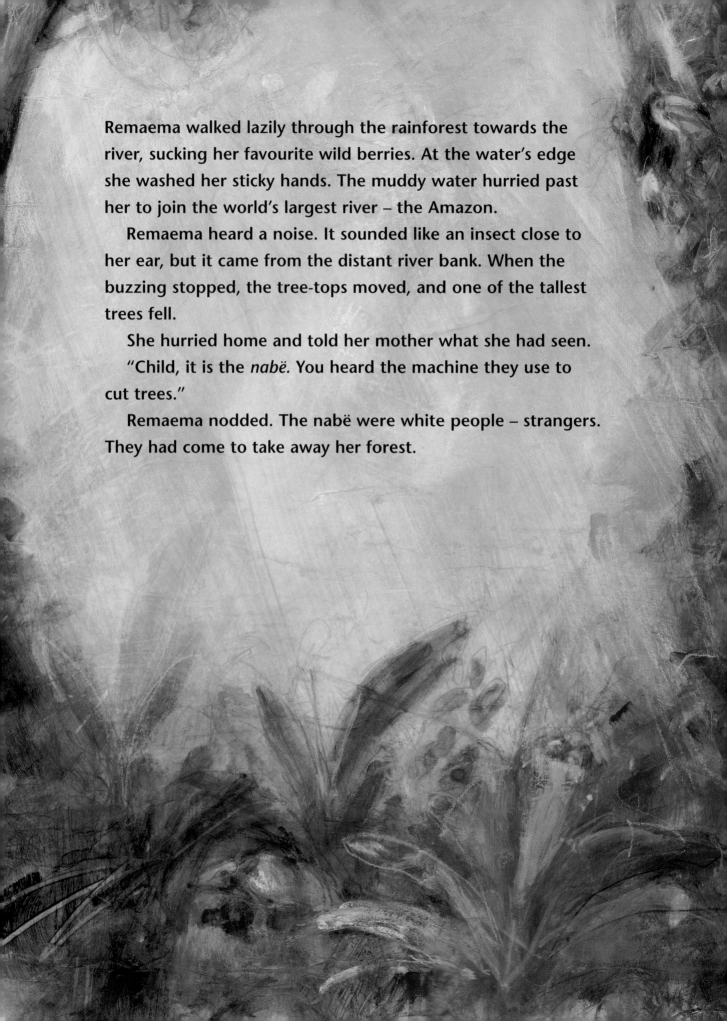

Remaema walked lazily through the rainforest towards the river, sucking her favourite wild berries. At the water's edge she washed her sticky hands. The muddy water hurried past her to join the world's largest river – the Amazon.

Remaema heard a noise. It sounded like an insect close to her ear, but it came from the distant river bank. When the buzzing stopped, the tree-tops moved, and one of the tallest trees fell.

She hurried home and told her mother what she had seen.

"Child, it is the *nabë.* You heard the machine they use to cut trees."

Remaema nodded. The nabë were white people – strangers. They had come to take away her forest.

As the sun set, Remaema's uncle Moawa returned to the *yano* – the round house which all the families shared. He proudly carried a new *machete*, and wore a bright red T-shirt.

Remaema's father asked where he got such precious things.

"From the nabë," he replied.

"Brother, you are helping the nabë, who are cutting down our trees?"

8

"These people are powerful…" Moawa replied angrily. "They have guns. They can kill us before we get close enough to hit them with an arrow. If we give them what they want, they will reward us. If we don't help them, they will take it anyway."

Then everyone spoke at once and started arguing.

"STOP!"

Her grandfather's shout made Remaema jump. Everyone
went quiet. "I have travelled far, and I have seen the nabë
cutting down trees, destroying our world. If we help them,
we make our own ruin."

Moawa defended himself. "The forest will return: we make
clearings, too, for growing bananas
and *casava*. When we move on,
trees soon cover our gardens…"

"No!" The old man stopped him. "We make small clearings. But when the nabë come, they take away every tree. When all the trees have gone, the animals die. It is the animals that spread the seeds of the trees. No animals, no forest. No forest, no food. Then we will all starve."

Remaema's grandfather was right. To grow their plants, the farmers cut down trees and set fire to the forest.
They soon moved on, but the trees did not grow back.

The fires scared away the forest animals. Peccaries used to be common once, but after the nabë came, hunters no longer caught these tasty forest pigs. Many fruit trees had vanished, too. Finding enough food took much longer. Sometimes there was nothing at all.

The nabë needed the help of guides such as Moawa. They offered tools, clothes and money in exchange. But afterwards, the farmers only paid the guides half of what they had promised. Villagers tried to hunt down the nabë who had cheated them, but the farmers kept them away with their guns.

Then Remaema met a nabë who was not like the others.
She was washing, when the sound of a motor boat drifted
upriver. Remaema watched from the forest shadows.

A young woman began unloading.
Remaema started to creep away.

"Wait! Don't go!" To her surprise, Remaema
could understand the tall, blond woman's words.

"Take this…" The woman held out a shiny square.
It reflected Remaema's face like a puddle, only brighter.

"My name is Jane. Do you live near here? Can I meet
your family?"

"She asks a lot of questions," said Remaema's mother
later, turning the mirror in her hand. "Is this all she gave
you?" She could see that Remaema liked Jane, and she
told Remaema's father. He persuaded everyone to gather
in the yano to meet the woman.

Jane explained that she wanted to learn how forest people use plants to treat disease.

But an angry shout interrupted her: "You nabë are all alike! You take what you want, then disappear."

Jane's face became as red as *nara xihi* seeds. "No! I have come to save the forest and the plants and animals that live here," she said. "The people who are burning the trees do not know the value of what they are destroying.

You cannot live here without the forest. This alone is a good enough reason to protect the trees. But the forest plants and creatures you collect could help solve hunger and sick people in other parts of the world. To study them, we must save everything, for every tree or beast depends on all the others. We can't do it without your help. You understand the forest."

Jane's speech lasted a long time. Afterwards there was a silence. Then one of the tribe's elders stood up.

"Very well," he said. "We will help you."

The forest people helped Jane with her study for half a year.

Soon after she left, Remaema's brother was playing at warriors with other boys in the garden. Throwing himself to the ground as if struck by a poisoned arrow, he shouted playfully, "Yow! I am dying, but my children will destroy your village, and kill your children…"

Then another boy fell to the ground. At first, everyone laughed. But he did not get up. He just lay among the plantain trees, covered in sweat.

"I'm s-s-so c-cold" he shivered. They carried him back to his hammock in the yano and his mother, Bahimi, asked a *shaman* to cure him.

The old healer paced around the hammock, calling on the spirits causing the illness to leave the boy's body. Afterwards, the shaman said, "He has malaria. Until we mixed with the nabë we never caught this sickness. To cure him, you need to collect bitter vine bark."

Remaema went to look for the vine bark with Bahimi. After two days walking along the shady forest trails, they neared the place where the vines grew. But something wasn't right. Smoke in the air made Remaena cough.

Half an hour later, they stepped out from the trees into brilliant sunlight. The forest was gone! The ground was burned black as far as they could see.

Bahimi wept. Now her son would have to get better without vine bark to help him.

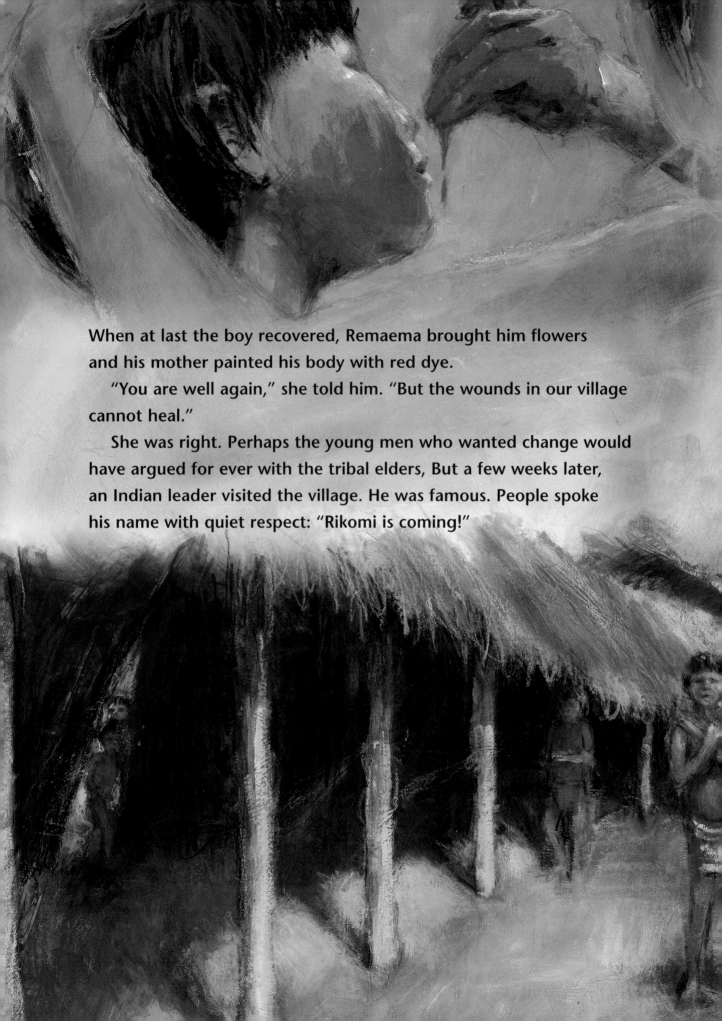

When at last the boy recovered, Remaema brought him flowers
and his mother painted his body with red dye.

"You are well again," she told him. "But the wounds in our village
cannot heal."

She was right. Perhaps the young men who wanted change would
have argued for ever with the tribal elders, But a few weeks later,
an Indian leader visited the village. He was famous. People spoke
his name with quiet respect: "Rikomi is coming!"

Like the villagers, Rikomi belonged to the Yanomami tribe,
but he wore shoes and worked for the government in the city.
Rikomi had not forgotten the battles he once fought against
the nabë farmers and miners. Remaema shivered when she saw
the scars on his body.

When Rikomi spoke to the grown-ups of the village,
Remaema listened too.

Swinging gently in a hammock, Rikomi spoke quietly.

"There doesn't have to be a fight between tradition and progress. Not everyone outside the forest wants to destroy it."

Remaema saw her father nod.

"Some nabë love the forest. You all know about Jane, who came to study healing plants. There are also tourists who want to visit the forest because it is home to half of all the Earth's living things."

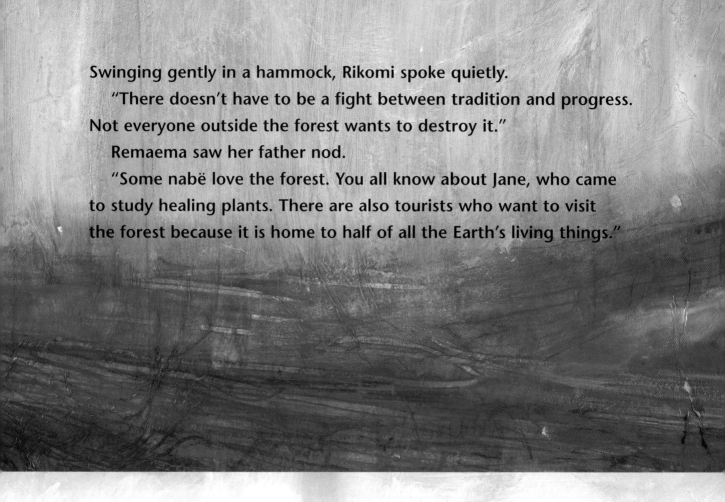

Another voice spoke. In a low chant an old warrior repeated, "My bow will kill them!"

The other villagers calmed the old man, and Rikomi went on, "Tourists could stay near the village, but not close enough to disturb life in the yano. We could show them the forest. Their money would pay for education and better health care, and for the government to keep nabë farmers away."

Eventually, everyone agreed – even Moawa.

A few months later, Remaema's uncle set off briskly
from the yano.

"Where are you going, Moawa?" asked Remaema..

"I'm off to find *yao nahi* trees for the visitors' house,"
he replied.

"But uncle, we already have plenty of logs."

"Ha! But we'll need stronger wood for the roof-beams,
and I know just where to find the trees." With that, Moawa
swaggered off into the forest, swinging his machete.

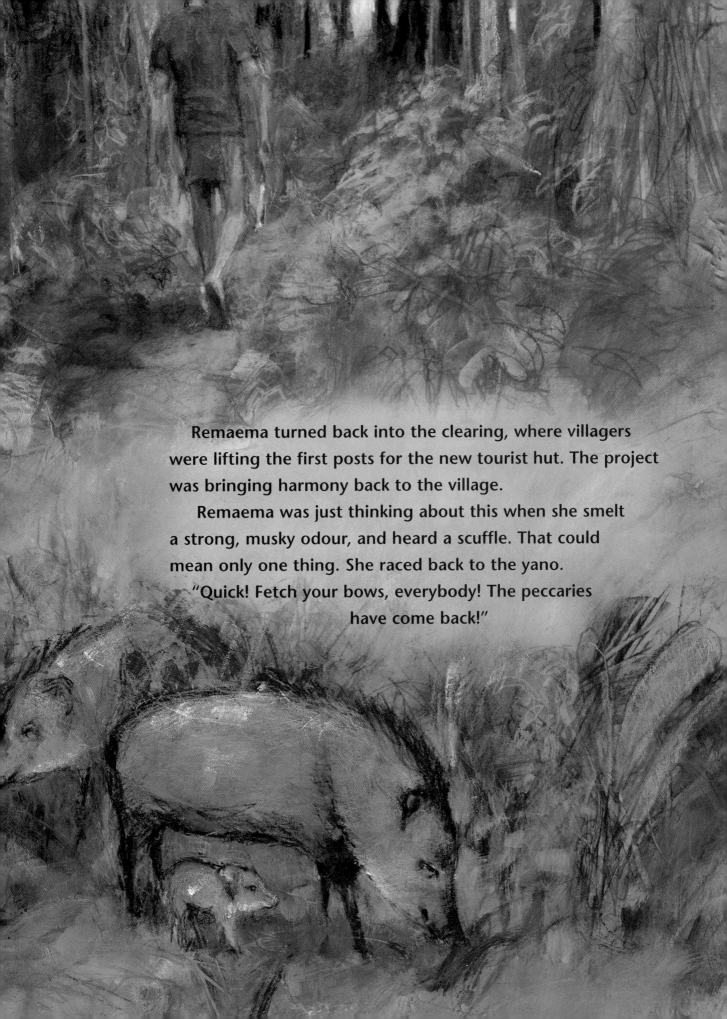

Remaema turned back into the clearing, where villagers were lifting the first posts for the new tourist hut. The project was bringing harmony back to the village.

Remaema was just thinking about this when she smelt a strong, musky odour, and heard a scuffle. That could mean only one thing. She raced back to the yano.

"Quick! Fetch your bows, everybody! The peccaries have come back!"

WHY RAINFORESTS MATTER

Rainforests once ringed the world like a belt. They covered much of the wettest land around the Earth's middle. The forests are shrinking fast. Nearly half have gone because people cut trees wastefully for timber or to make paper. Every second, timber workers cut down an area of rainforest as big as 16 tennis courts.

Jane, the scientist in the story, knows that we must preserve the rainforest because of the huge variety of useful and beautiful plants and animals that live there. For each kind of rainforest plant that scientists have found and named, there may be as many as six more yet to be discovered. Forest people are the only ones who know how to make food or healing drugs from these plants. Some South American groups use as many as 1300 different plants.

But there is another reason for preserving the world's great rainforests. They control our planet's climate, its weather pattern. The trees soak up waste gasses that pollute the atmosphere. Cutting down the trees frees the gasses. This changes the climate, making it hotter and stormier.

By preserving the rainforests and the plants, people and other animals they contain, we are safeguarding our own health – and the health of our planet.

GLOSSARY

casava (page 10): Food plant with large fleshy roots used for making flour.

machete (pages 8, 26): Light axe used for cutting small trees.

nabë (pages 6, 8, 10, 11, 13, 14, 16, 19, 23, 24): Yanomami name for white people or strangers.

nara xihi (page 18): Yanomami name for a forest plant collected for the bright red dye on its seeds.

peccary (pages 13, 27): Small, fierce, forest pig hunted for food.

rainforest (page 28): Dense woodland growing in some of the warmest, wettest parts of the world.

shaman (page 19): Healer-priest who talks to ghosts and gods, following their advice to cure ills and perform magic.

yano (pages 8, 15, 24, 26, 27): Yanomami word for a large, circular forest shelter where many families live together.

Yanomami tribe: The people in this book – a Native South American people who live in the rainforests of south Venezuela and north Brazil.

yao nahi (page 26): Forest tree with a very strong trunk, used for building.

OTHER PICTURE BOOKS IN PAPERBACK FROM FRANCES LINCOLN

B IS FOR BRAZIL
Maria de Fatima Campos

From *Carnival* to *Guarana*, from *Football* to *Zebu*, here is a celebration of Brazil
in all its cultural diversity. Maria de Fatima Campos illustrates the contrasts
between city and rainforest and the vibrant world of Brazilian children –
at home, at school, fishing on the river and painting in the open air.
ISBN 0-7112-1479-4

HOW GREEN ARE YOU?
David Bellamy
Illustrated by Penny Dann

Can a six year-old help to save the world?
Renowned conservationist David Bellamy says yes!
In this fun and informative book, the Friendly Whale leads us
on a tour of our every-day habitat, explaining how we can
protect the environment at every step.
ISBN 0-7112-0679-1

THE DROP IN MY DRINK –
The Story of Water on our Planet
Meredith Hooper
Illustrated by Chris Coady

The intriguing story of a drop of water, from the beginnings
of our planet to the water cycle of today.
ISBN 0-7112-1182-5

Frances Lincoln titles are available from all good bookshops.
You can also buy books and find out more about your favourite titles,
authors and illustrators at our website:
www.franceslincoln.com.